THE SUGARING-OFF PARTY

D1294099

BUREAU DE POSTE
SAINT-HILAIRE
1854
BOULANGERIE
TARTES
GATEAUX

JONATHAN LONDON

paintings by GILLES PELLETIER

LESTER PUBLISHING LIMITED

First published in Canada in 1995 by Lester Publishing Limited,
56 The Esplanade, Toronto, Canada M5E 1A7
Originally published in the United States in 1995 by Dutton Children's Books,
a division of Penguin Books USA Inc., New York

Text copyright © 1995 by Jonathan London
Illustrations copyright © 1995 by Gilles Pelletier

All rights reserved. No part of this work covered by the copyrights hereon may be reproduced or used in any form or by any means—graphic, electronic or mechanical, including photocopying, recording, taping or information storage and retrieval systems—without the prior written permission of the publisher or, in the case of photocopying or other reprographic copying, a licence from the Canadian Reprography Collective.

Canadian Cataloging in Publication Data

London, Jonathan, 1947-
The sugaring-off party

ISBN 1-895555-84-1 (bound) ISBN 1-895555-89-2 (pbk.)

I. Pelletier, Gilles, 1946- . II. Title.

PZ7.L8432Su 1995 j813'.54 C94-931791-8

Designed by Adrian Leichter

Printed in Hong Kong

96 97 98 99 5 4 3 2 1

for my wife, Maureen; our sons, Aaron and Sean;
their "Grand-mère" Catherine Weisenberger, née Francoeur;
and for their "Tante Loulou," Lorraine

with many thanks to Chris Bolger, John Richardson,
Jeanne Modesitt, and Louise Woodfine

J. L.

for my wife, Linda, my favorite art critic

G. P.

"It looks like a Sugar Moon tonight," says Grand-mère, looking out the window. "And tomorrow, *mon petit chou,* should be a fine day for the party."

Every March, for many, many years, the family has driven out to a maple sugaring in the country. But tomorrow will be Paul's very first time.

"Grand-mère, can you tell me about your first sugaring-off, long ago?"

"Of course, my dear." Paul's grandmother is sprightly for a woman her age. In the firelight, with her bird-fragile bones, she looks almost like a little girl. She flops down on the sofa and pats the cushion beside her. "Come. Sit beside me, *mon petit chou*."

Paul snuggles close and gazes into the fire. He loves Grand-mère's stories. Even the shadows lean down to listen. . . .

When I was a little girl, just your age, my parents and sisters and I rode out to Tante Loulou's sugar bush—a maple-sugar forest. My aunt Loulou lived not far from Montréal, near the village of Mont-Saint-Hilaire. Her family had a sugar shack there, where they boiled maple sap down into sugar and syrup. In French, a sugar shack is called *la cabane à sucre,* and that's what a sugaring-off party is called, too. The party was our way of celebrating the coming of spring after a long, cold winter.

We were all singers in our family, and we went by sleigh, singing folk songs all the way. About sweethearts and horses and heroes. And *Alouette*—you know that one!

Alouette, gentille alouette.
Alouette, je te plumerai! . . .

The snow lay on the stubby fields, thawing by day, freezing by night. Here and there, bare patches released the smell of earth. In the woods, clumps of melting snow fell softly off the trees, and branches dripped. But beneath the covered bridges we crossed, the brooks still crackled with ice.

Neighbors came from all around—some on skis or snowshoes; some by sled or horse-drawn wagon. When we reached *la cabane à sucre,* just down the sugar road from Tante Loulou's farmhouse, three or four families had already arrived. I spied my terrible twin cousins, Richard and Robert, in the crowd.

But jolly Tante Loulou greeted all of us with hearty shouts and gave Mama a great big hug. My aunt's hair was curled tight to her head like a wool cap, and her eyes danced with laughter. She was my favorite relative then, *mon petit chou*. Mama took the heavy basket of homemade muffins and jams from my lap. Then Tante Loulou lifted me up high out of the sleigh with her strong arms.

LA CABANE
A
LOU LOU

While Mama and Papa chatted with the grown-ups, my two older sisters and I scampered over to the maple trees with our cousins. We flapped the tin hats on the sap buckets that hung on the trees and poked our fingers inside for a taste. Tante Loulou had told us that *la tire,* the taffy made from maple syrup poured on snow, was the sweetest treat in the world. But the sap in the buckets was still thin and green and woody tasting. We didn't know that it would only turn sweet later, after it had been boiled down into syrup.

We children raced around, grabbing scarves and dunking snow down each other's backs. My boots got stuck in the mud, and the twins—those little devils—pushed me all the way in! Your great-aunts, my sisters, had to tug me out. Richard and Robert were laughing, but then we girls pushed *them* in, and it was *our* turn to laugh! I've always been tiny, but tough, too. By the time Mama called us in to eat, we were hungry walking mud puddles, slowly turning to ice.

Inside the sugar shack, it was steamy warm from the maple syrup—*le sirop d'érable*—which was boiling in long pans on the big wood stove. It takes forty gallons of sap to make just one gallon of syrup, you see. The more you boil it, the thicker and sweeter it gets! And when the water boils all the way down, maple sugar is left. But just before that, when the syrup is extra thick, it's perfect for pouring on snow and making *la tire*. We kept asking Mama, "When can we have *la tire?* When, Mama, when?"

"First eat dinner," she would say. "Then we'll see." *La tire* was for dessert.

Tante Loulou was in charge of the kitchen. Trays of hard rolls shuttled in and out of ovens. Plates clattered. Folks clomped in with a flutter of snow, stamping their feet. Even when the door was shut, you could feel the cold air slipping in through cracks in the walls and mingling with the steam. Big pots of beans with back bacon simmered in maple syrup on the wood stove. Potatoes, too. And eggs sizzled in syrup, along with pancakes stuffed with bacon. The thick, rich smell of the bubbling, tumbling, boiling syrup filled the air.

FESTIVAL DE LA POMME ST HILAIRE

All the children sat down at our table. My stomach growled. I banged my spoon, and Mama hushed me. Then Richard and Robert banged their spoons loud, but one glance from Tante Loulou stopped them cold.

At last, the feast began. *"Allons manger!"* boomed Papa. Let's eat! And we dug into our heaps of beans and bacon, our eggs, potatoes, and pancakes. We chomped on brown bread and hard rolls, dipping pieces into the maple syrup sauce, pushing them round and round our plates. One of my braids fell into the syrup, and the tip got stiff as an old paintbrush. I dunked it in Richard's coffee cup when he wasn't looking. He'd snuck the coffee, anyway. All the rest of us were drinking hot apple cider.

While we feasted, folks with fiddles and an accordion played joyous tunes. After eating, I helped push aside the long plank tables to clear a place for dancing.

I clapped along as some old-timers did the step dance, stomping their boots on the boards in a kind of jig, while others clicked out the rhythm with pairs of spoons. *Clickety-clack* went heels against floorboards. *Clackety-click* went spoons against thighs. A few more dancers joined in, linking arms. *"Tout le monde danse!"* shouted Tante Loulou. So everyone got up to dance!

I watched and clapped and tapped my feet . . . until I found myself swept in! Round and round, I dipped and swung, spun and swirled, stomped and skipped and yipped with joy . . .

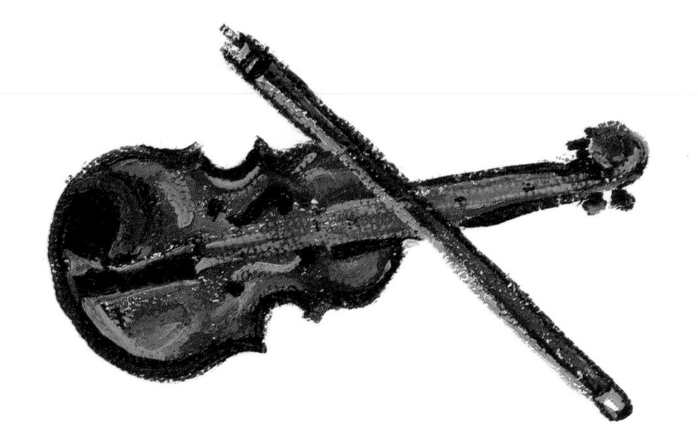

CHEZ
LOULOU

till the room whirled, and down I crashed. I laughed so hard I could barely breathe.

Tante Loulou helped me up. She was laughing, too. Then she said something. Over the noise, all I could hear was *"la tire."* I'd been having so much fun, I almost forgot!

As my sisters and I bundled into our mud-caked coats and pulled on our pointy wool *tuques,* I kept thinking, "The troughs are waiting. . . . The troughs are waiting for us. . . ."

"Allons-y!" we shouted. Let's go! And we rushed outside.

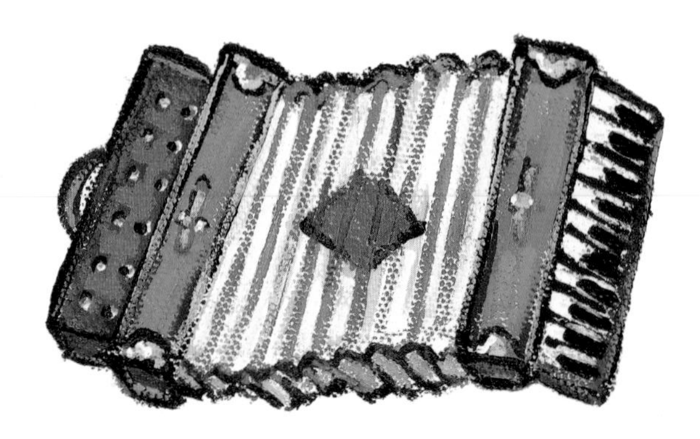

The twins, of course, had cut in front, elbows flying. But after them, we were first in line. Tante Loulou handed out paddle sticks. I waited my turn. My mouth watered, and I licked my lips.

Suddenly a ruckus broke out. Richard bonked Robert with his paddle stick, and Robert bonked him back. Tante Loulou could laugh over just about anything, but her eyes were cold as she pointed the twins to the back of the line.

Now we were first! I couldn't believe it.

When my turn came, Tante Loulou, eyes twinkling again, ladled out the boiled-down syrup. It trickled down, all thick and steamy, burning a waxy golden line in the white snow.

I pressed my paddle stick in and twisted it round and round. Out came a great maple-taffy snowsicle—*la tire!* Mmmm. I munched and crunched and licked the chewy treat. Tante Loulou was right. There's nothing in the whole world sweeter than *la tire!*

I was stuffed, but my sister Michelle and I kept coming back for more. My sister Louise was still on her first one, taking sharp licks with her tidy little tongue. Richard and Robert kept coming back for more, too, until their father finally got mad. The last I saw of them, the terrible twins were being carried off in their papa's arms, kicking and squealing like pigs.

It was getting late. Just as my head was ringing from all the sweetness, I felt Tante Loulou's strong arms lift me up. She buried me in a hug as deep as forever and set me down carefully in our sleigh.

Holding my cheeks in her hands, she said, "You must come back next year, my little dancer with the big appetite. It's a tradition, *n'est-ce pas?* And we must keep our traditions alive." Then she gave me a fat kiss on both my cheeks.

As we pulled away in the sleigh, Tante Loulou kept blowing kisses and waving. "*Au revoir,* Tante Loulou!" we called. Good-bye!

Gliding back down the sugar road, the dark branches of the maples arching over us, my sisters and I chattered about the party. What fun it had been! "Can we go again next year, Papa?" I asked. "Please?"

Papa growled, "Ask your mama." But then he winked.

"Tante Loulou says it's a tradition, Mama. She says we've just got to come back next year for *la tire.*"

"Whatever your papa says, *mon petit chou.*" (She called me little cabbage, too, Paul, like I call you.) Then I saw Mama wink, right back at Papa.

Well, little did I know that night that I would someday see my sixtieth celebration of *la cabane à sucre,* the sugaring-off party! Yes, tomorrow will be my sixtieth party!

But that night, long ago, I just snuggled deep beneath our bearskin rug as the darkness fell. Half-asleep but full of joy, I watched as the moon rose…

LA CABANE

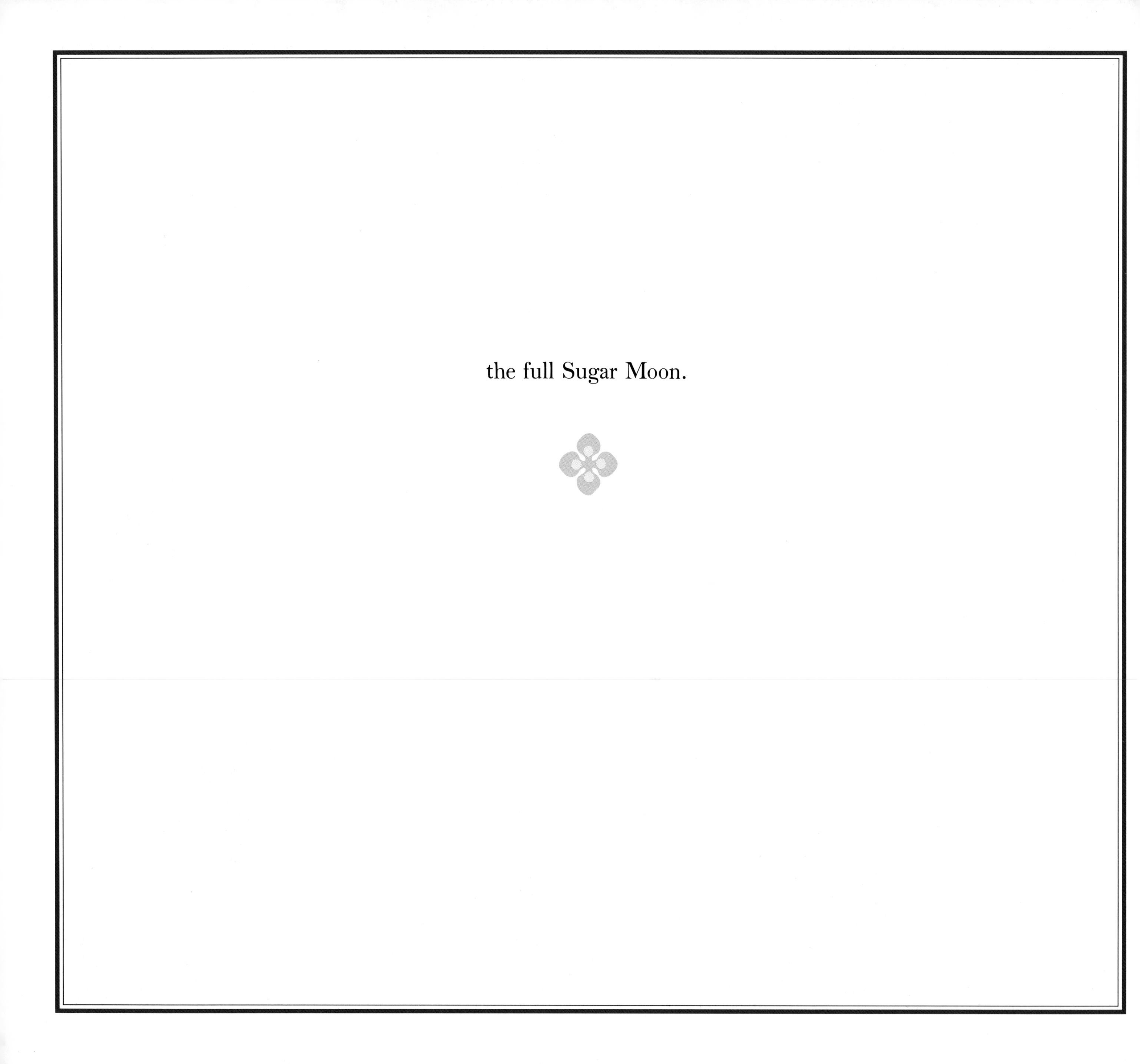

the full Sugar Moon.

• GLOSSARY •

Allons manger Let's eat
Allons-y Let's go
Au revoir Good-bye
la cabane à sucre the sugar shack; also, the sugaring-off party
grand-mère grandmother
mon petit chou literally, *my little cabbage*; an endearment akin to *my little darling*
N'est-ce pas? Isn't that so?
le sirop d'érable maple syrup
la tante aunt
la tire the sticky, gooey maple syrup that is poured on the snow; also, the taffy that is the outcome of this process. (From the verb *tirer*, meaning "to pull." The complete French phrase for the syrup on the snow is: *la tire sur la neige*.)
Tout le monde danse! Everybody dance!
la tuque a pointy wool hat

• SUGAR MOON •

or Maple Sugar Moon, is what the Abenaki Indians call the March moon, because early spring is the time for maple sugaring. The Abenaki people are native to Maine and southern Québec, as well as to Vermont.

• ALOUETTE •

Alouette, gentille alouette.	Little lark, nice little lark.
Alouette, je te plumerai!	Little lark, I'll pluck your feathers off!
Je te plumerai la tête,	I'll pluck the feathers off your head,
Je te plumerai la tête.	I'll pluck the feathers off your head.
Et la tête!	And your head!
Et la tête!	And your head!
Alouette!	Little lark!
Alouette!	Little lark!

(Verse repeats, with feathers plucked from different parts of the lark's body each time.)